For school staff everywhere,
but especially to Anson School, Cricklewood –
to whom I owe my sanity.
– *E.L.*

First published in Great Britain in 1994 by Magi Publications
55 Crowland Avenue, Hayes, Middlesex UB3 4JP

Text © 1994 by Ewa Lipniacka
Illustrations © 1994 by Jennifer Bell

The right of Ewa Lipniacka to be identified as the author
of this work has been asserted by her in accordance with
The Copyright, Designs and Patents Act 1988.

Printed and bound in Hong Kong
Produced by Mandarin Offset

ISBN 1 85430 256 6

The Trouble with Trainers

Written by Ewa Lipniacka
Illustrated by Jennifer Bell

Magi Publications, London

The world of fashion passed Curlywood School by until Pepe's seventh birthday, when he received a new computer game, a nice vest from Aunt Lucy – and a magnificent pair of trainers.

Pepe wore them to school straight away.
His teacher didn't seem quite so impressed
as his friends were.

Ahmed's birthday was next, and his trainers were even bigger and better; Asha's were so splendid that the boys invited her to join their gang.

"I'll think about it," she said.

What no one realised was that trainers spelt trouble ...

Damien didn't speak to his mother for a week, because she wouldn't buy him any trainers. Robert's were rather a disappointment, but then he should never have asked his granny to get them for him . . .

Soon the class was split right down the middle.
The Trainer Gang was those who had trainers, and the
rest, those who would not be seen dead in them.
Best friends ignored each other . . .
Team games became impossible . . .

Until finally Mrs Whackett,
the Play Lady, decided that

SOMETHING HAD TO BE DONE.

The Head Teacher called a meeting of all the teachers, the dinner ladies, the governors, the parents, the caretaker, Mr Jones the lollipop man, and Mrs Whackett –

BUT NO CHILDREN WERE ALLOWED.

"The question is," said the Head.
"Are trainers a good thing or a bad thing?"

Everyone had something to say.
Soon all the adults were as divided as the children,
and there seemed to be no solution to the problem.
Then suddenly Mrs Whackett had an idea.

"A Sports Competition!" said Mrs Whackett.
"The Trainer Gang against the Rest. That should decide it."
"Good idea," everyone agreed.

Everyone wanted to help.
Mr Bellow, the Woodwork Teacher, said he would
build a magnificent assault course.

Miss Hale, the P.E. Teacher, and the Dinner Ladies
all helped Mrs Whackett design the invitations, and the
Parent Staff Association even bought some prizes.

On the day of the Competition the crowds gathered,
the teams lined up, and everyone prepared for battle . . .

Damien, whose mother never had bought him a pair, turned up in his sister's trainers and joined the Trainer Gang. "That's not fair," said the others, but Rachel reminded them that he was rotten at sports anyway and no great loss.

Mr Jones waved his starter's lollipop for the first
race and they were off!
And that was when the Trainer Gang discovered
the trouble with trainers . . .

Damien was the first to part with one of his trainers
but then he should have realised his sister's feet
were bigger than his . . .

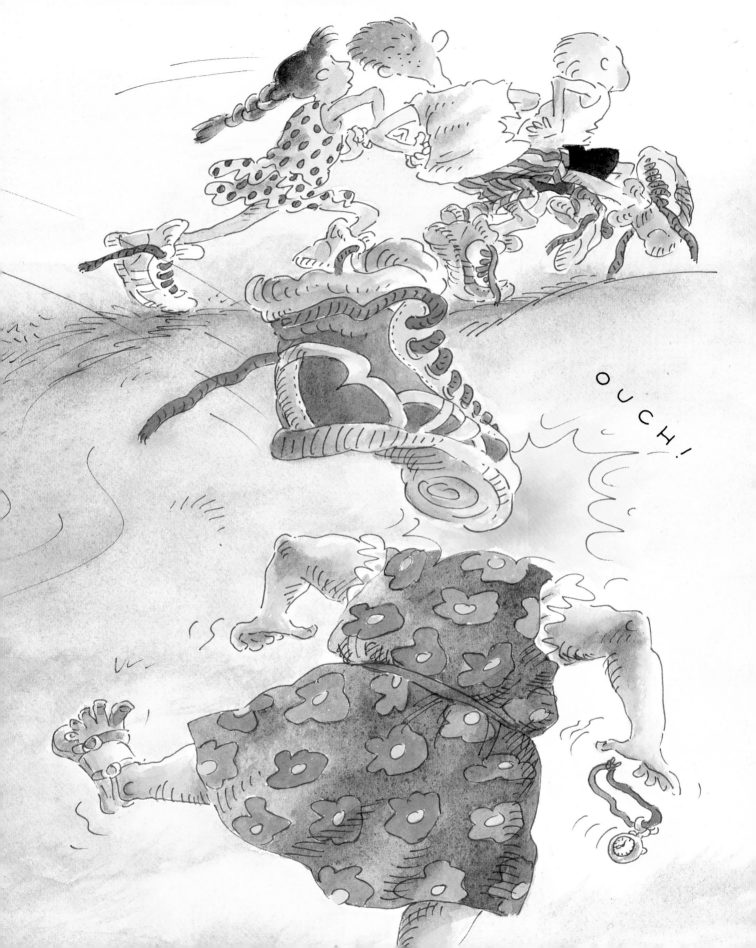

OUCH!

And no one had thought to warn the hot air
balloonists about high flying trainers during the
trampoline event . . .

The long jump brought a lovely surprise to Mr Green
next door . . .

. . . and it took till the next morning to untangle some of the runners in the three-legged race.

"That will teach them not to be slaves to fashion," muttered the grown-ups in sensible voices. "Well, that's probably the last we'll hear of trainers."

"Silly things, trainers," Pepe announced the next morning to his ex-Trainer gang. "Now what I really fancy is one of those little rucksacks. They really *do* look great!"